Vidia

and the

Fairy

Crown

Vidia
and the
Fairy Crown

WRITTEN BY
LAURA DRISCOLL

ILLUSTRATED BY
JUDITH HOLMES CLARKE
& THE DISNEY STORYBOOK ARTISTS

A STEPPING STONE BOOK™
RANDOM HOUSE 🏠 NEW YORK

Library of Congress Cataloging-in-Publication Data

Driscoll, Laura.
Vidia and the fairy crown / written by Laura Driscoll; illustrated by Judith Holmes Clarke.
p. cm.
"A Stepping Stone book."
SUMMARY: When Vidia, a disagreeable fairy, finds herself accused of stealing the Queen's tiara, she enlists the aid of a fellow fairy to help investigate and the two race against time to clear Vidia's name.

ISBN 0-7364-2372-9 (pbk.)

[1. Fairies—Fiction. 2. Stealing—Fiction. 3. Lost and found possessions—Fiction.] I. Clarke, Judith, ill. II. Title.
PZ7.D79Vid 2006   [E]—dc22
2005004833

www.randomhouse.com/kids/disney
Printed in the United States of America

All About Fairies

IF YOU HEAD toward the second star on your right and fly straight on till morning, you'll come to Never Land, a magical island where mermaids play and children never grow up.

When you arrive, you might hear something like the tinkling of little bells. Follow that sound and you'll find Pixie Hollow, the secret heart of Never Land.

A great old maple tree grows in Pixie Hollow, and in it live hundreds of fairies and sparrow men. Some of them can do water magic, others can fly like the wind, and still others can speak to animals. You see, Pixie Hollow is the Never fairies' kingdom, and each fairy who lives there has a special, extraordinary talent.

Not far from the Home Tree, nestled in the branches of a hawthorn, is Mother Dove, the most magical creature of all. She sits on her egg, watching over the fairies, who in turn watch over her. For as long as Mother Dove's egg stays well and whole, no one in Never Land will ever grow old.

Once, Mother Dove's egg *was* broken. But we are not telling the story of the egg here. Now it is time for Vidia's tale. . . .

Vidia

and the

Fairy

Crown

❧

Come one, come every Never fairy
and every sparrow man to
Her Royal Majesty Queen Clarion's
Arrival Day Bash!

·· where ··

The Home Tree Dining Hall

·· when ··

The evening of the next full
moon, just after sunset

To make it the merriest, wear your fairy best!

❧

EVERY FAIRY AND sparrow man in Pixie
Hollow had received the same invitation. It
was handwritten on linen in blackberry juice.

It was going to be the biggest celebration Pixie Hollow had seen in a long time.
So, on the day of the party, the Home Tree
was abuzz with activity. The Never fairies
went all out getting ready to celebrate the
Arrival Day of their beloved queen,
Clarion, whose nickname was Ree.

In the kitchen, on the ground floor of the Home Tree, the cooking- and baking-talent fairies were whipping up the seven-course royal Arrival Day dinner. The menu included dandelion leaves stuffed with rice, pine nuts, and spices; oven-roasted minipumpkin soup; and potpies filled with dwarf mushrooms and mouse Brie. Dulcie, a baking-talent fairy, was churning out batch after batch of her specialty, the most delicious poppy puff rolls in all of Never Land. And for dessert, she made a ten-layer raspberry-vanilla cake with buttercream frosting.

Meanwhile, the polishing-talent fairies were hard at work in the Home Tree lobby and the dining hall. Every brass plate, every doorknob, mirror, window latch, and marble floor tile was polished until the fairies could see their reflections just about everywhere they looked.

The decoration-talent fairies and the celebration-setup fairies zipped about the dining hall. They moved the tables and chairs. They draped the tables with gold tablecloths and delicate lacy spiderwebs. They sprinkled flower-petal confetti on every table and across the floor. They hung colorful balloons in the arched doorway.

The light-talent fairies did double duty. Some of them set up the firefly lanterns that would fill the room with thousands of dancing points of light. Others did a practice run of the light show they would perform for the queen at the party. They skillfully flared and dimmed their fairy glows to create a dazzling display.

The sewing-talent fairies were putting

the finishing touches on the queen's dress. It was a full-length masterpiece of the finest silk, decorated with pale pink rose petals, the softest green leaves, and freshwater pearls.

Even Tinker Bell, a member of the pots-and-pans talent, was helping out. The cooking-talent fairies needed every pot and pan they could get their hands on. So Tinker Bell had risen early that morning. She finished fixing all the broken pots in her workshop on the second floor of the Home Tree. Then she returned them all, making several trips between her workshop and the kitchen.

On her last trip down to the kitchen, Tink met up with her friend Rani, a water-talent fairy. Rani had been working in the kitchen all morning long. She was using her talent to help out with lots of little

tasks, like getting the water to boil faster on the stove.

"Rani!" Tink called. "Do you have time for a break?"

Rani looked around the kitchen. Things seemed to be running smoothly. She didn't think she'd be missed if she stepped out for a few minutes.

"Yes," Rani replied. "I do have time. Let's go out back and whistle for Brother Dove. Maybe he can fly us down to the beach."

Rani did not have wings, you see. She was the only Never fairy who didn't. She had given them up to save Mother Dove's egg—and Pixie Hollow itself. Ever since then, Brother Dove had been her wings. Whenever she wanted or needed to fly somewhere, Rani just whistled for him, and Brother Dove came to her.

Tinker Bell and Rani left the kitchen through the back door. They stepped out into the late-morning sunshine. It was a glorious, clear day.

Tink took a deep breath of fresh air. "It's going to be a beautiful—"

"—evening," said Rani, finishing the thought. She had a habit of finishing others' sentences. "The perfect night for a party."

Just then, there was a rustling in the brush overhead. Both Tink and Rani jumped.

"Is it a hawk?" Rani cried in alarm. Hungry hawks were the greatest threats to the Never fairies' safety.

Instinctively, Tink flew in front of Rani, shielding her. She strained her eyes and gazed up into the brush. She wanted to get a better look.

Then, as she made out the shape of a fairy among the leaves, Tinker Bell relaxed. She put her hands on her hips.

"That's no hawk," Tink said with a laugh. "It's Vidia."

A dark-haired fairy zipped down from above. She landed next to Tink and Rani. "Hello, darlings," Vidia said. She flashed them a sly smile. Vidia threw around words like "darling," "dear," and "sweetheart." But the way she said them made her fellow fairies wonder if she meant the opposite. "Why aren't you two inside getting ready for the big party—just like all the other good fairies? Hmm?" Vidia asked them.

"We were," Tinker Bell replied shortly. "We're—"

"—taking a break," said Rani.

"What's *your* excuse?" Tinker Bell asked Vidia.

Tinker Bell knew all too well that Vidia wouldn't be caught dead helping out that day. Vidia's relationship with Queen Ree was . . . complicated. In fact, Vidia's relationship with everyone in Pixie Hollow was complicated. She was the fastest of the fast-flying-talent fairies. But one day, Vidia had decided that being the fastest was not fast enough. Greedy for even more speed, she had done something cruel. She had plucked ten feathers from Mother Dove. Then she had ground those feathers into extra-powerful fairy dust that gave her extra flying speed.

After that, Queen Ree decided that Vidia couldn't be trusted around Mother Dove. She banned Vidia from Mother Dove's company. Over time, Vidia had become more and more distant with the other fairies. She was the only fairy in Pixie Hollow who didn't live in the Home Tree. Instead, Vidia lived on her own in a sour-plum tree. Truthfully, most of the fairies and sparrow men thought that a little distance between them and Vidia was not a bad thing.

"Are you even *coming* to the party tonight?" Tinker Bell asked Vidia.

Vidia smiled. "To the queen's party?" She laughed mockingly. "Of course not, dear. Why, that's what I'd call a waste of a perfectly good evening." Vidia paused and seemed to consider a new thought. "Oh, unless you need someone to fly in and snatch that gaudy crown off high and mighty Queen Ree's head," she said. "Now, *that* sounds like fun. In fact, that's quite a tempting idea—party or no party." Vidia shrugged. "Ah, well. You two dears have fun tonight!"

With that, Vidia took to the air. In a flash, she was gone.

Tinker Bell and Rani looked at each other and shook their heads.

That evening, as the sun inched its way toward the horizon, the activity in the fairy queen's chambers inside the Home Tree kicked into high gear. The queen's four helper fairies—Cinda, Rhia, Lisel, and Grace—were laying out the clothes, shoes, and jewelry that Ree would wear to the party.

Lisel gently carried the queen's fancy new gown from the closet and put it on the queen's bed. She unbuttoned the five pearl buttons to make it easier to help the queen dress later.

Grace picked out a pair of pointy-toed, rose-colored silk heels for the queen to wear. She placed them near the foot of the bed.

Rhia opened the queen's jewelry box. She chose a pretty shell charm on a silver chain that went nicely with the queen's dress.

Meanwhile, Cinda entered the queen's sitting room and crossed to the crown cabinet on a side table. Naturally, the queen would wear her crown to the party. Not only was it incredibly beautiful, but also, it was tradition for the queen to wear the crown to any celebration. The crown was the most special fairy treasure in all of Pixie Hollow. Except for Mother Dove's egg, it was the only item that the fairies still had from the earliest days of the Never fairies. It had been passed down from fairy queen to fairy queen throughout the ages. It was priceless and irreplaceable.

So when she opened the cabinet, Cinda froze.

The crown wasn't there.

2

WHEN QUEEN REE heard the news of the missing crown, she called an emergency meeting. Twenty-five message-talent fairies zipped out of the Home Tree. They fanned out in all directions to ask every fairy and sparrow man in Pixie Hollow to gather immediately in the Home Tree courtyard.

Queen Ree waited patiently. She

watched as, by ones and twos and threes, fairies flew into the clearing. Many of them looked worried and whispered to one another nervously.

"What do you think is wrong?" whispered one fairy.

"It must be an emergency," whispered another, "or it wouldn't be called an emergency meeting."

"The queen *does* look very serious," whispered a sparrow man.

They gathered in a wide circle around Ree. Some fairies hovered in midair. Some found standing room on the mossy ground. Some sat on toadstools or small pebbles. Everyone had his or her eyes fixed on the queen, who waited silently as the crowd and the hubbub grew.

Soon the courtyard was bright with the glows of hundreds of Never fairies and sparrow men. Even Vidia was there. She lurked in the shadows of a mulberry bush. At last, when Ree judged that everyone was present, she cleared her throat. All of the fairies and sparrow men fell silent.

"Fairies! Sparrow men!" the queen called out. "I have called this meeting to let you all know that there will be no celebration tonight."

A murmur arose from the crowd. The fairies exchanged puzzled glances. No Arrival Day celebration? After all the planning and preparation?

"I need your help in finding my crown, which has gone missing today," the queen went on. At that, the crowd's murmur became a cry of alarm. The crown . . . missing! Every Never fairy and sparrow man knew the crown's history. But what did this mean? What had happened to the crown?

"Do you mean that someone has *stolen* the crown?" Tink called out from her perch on a tree root.

"Now, now," said the queen, trying to calm the crowd. "Let's not jump to any conclusions. There's probably a good explanation for why the crown isn't where it's supposed to be. And if we all work together, I'm sure we'll find it."

"Well, where was it last seen?" asked Terence, a fairy-dust-talent sparrow man.

"Who was the last fairy to see it?" added Tink.

"How long has it been gone?" asked Iridessa, a light-talent fairy.

Queen Ree held up her hands to quiet the crowd. "Those are all good questions," she said. "Not all of them have answers yet. But maybe I should ask my helper fairy Cinda to come forward. She is the fairy who noticed that the crown was missing. After you hear what she has to say, you will know as much about all of this as I do."

Cinda sat with her talent in the front row of the ring of fairies. Her glow flared with embarrassment as she met the queen's eyes. "Don't be afraid, dear," the queen said. She waved Cinda over. "Just tell everyone what you told me."

Slowly, hesitantly, Cinda flew to the center of the courtyard and stood at the queen's side.

"Well, there's not much to tell," she said quietly. She told everyone how shocked she'd been when she found the crown cabinet empty earlier that evening. "I thought maybe another fairy had beaten me to it—had already taken the crown out and laid it on the queen's dressing table. But when I asked the others if they knew where the crown was, no one did!" Cinda looked up at the queen. "We didn't know what to do! Nothing like this has ever happened before! So we told the queen about it right away. She called the emergency meeting . . . and here we are."

Queen Ree smiled at her. "Thank you, Cinda," she said. Then, as Cinda retook her place in the circle of fairies, the queen looked up at the crowd. "Now I have something to ask all of you," she said. "I would like you to think back over the last couple of days. Has anyone seen or heard or done anything that might have something to do with the missing crown?"

No one spoke for a long while. The fairies all looked expectantly around the circle. Their eyes darted this way and that, following the smallest noise—the slightest cough, rustle, or sigh—only to find that the fairy who made it didn't have anything to say after all.

Then, at last, a tiny voice piped up from a cluster of toadstools near the Home Tree front door.

"Queen Ree," said Florian, a grass-weaving fairy, "I saw the crown yesterday."

"You did?" the queen replied excitedly. "Where? When?" Every fairy and sparrow man held his or her breath, waiting to hear Florian's reply.

"Well, you were wearing it," she said, "at afternoon tea in the tearoom."

The crowd let out a sigh of disappointment.

"Yes, yes, Florian," snapped Vidia. "Who *didn't* see her wearing the crown yesterday at tea? That's not the kind of information we need."

The queen turned to Vidia. "That's quite enough, Vidia," she scolded. "Florian was only trying to be helpful."

"Yeah, Vidia," said Rani. She hopped off her seat on a pebble and put her hands on her hips. "Besides, I remember you making a certain nasty comment about the crown this morning. What was it you said, exactly?"

Tink chimed in before Vidia could

answer. "She said she was planning to fly into Queen Ree's party and snatch the crown off her head."

All eyes turned toward Vidia, who crossed her arms and shifted her weight

from one foot to the other. She scowled across the fairy circle at Rani and Tink.

"Well?" said Queen Ree, turning to look at Vidia. "Is that true? Did you say that, Vidia?"

"I said that I wasn't coming to the party," Vidia replied. "I think my exact words were 'unless, of course, you need someone to fly in and snatch that gaudy crown off high and mighty Queen Ree's head.'"

The crowd gasped. To say such a thing—and right in front of the queen herself! But then again, Vidia had never been one to mince words.

"That's not all," Tinker Bell said. "Then you said that the idea of snatching the crown sounded like fun—that it was something to consider—"

"—party or no party," said Rani, finishing Tink's sentence. "It's true. She said that, too."

The crowd gasped again.

Vidia forced a laugh. "Oh, this is ridiculous," she said. "Yes, I said those things. But, really, what would I want with your crown, Ree? What would I do with it? It's not like I could steal it and then fly around wearing it, could I?"

Queen Ree looked troubled. "No, Vidia," she replied. "That doesn't make sense. Honestly, I have no idea what you would want with the crown. And honestly, I don't want to believe that you had anything to do with its disappearance. But these are serious charges."

The queen looked around at all the

fairies and sparrow men. "Does anyone else have any other information to share?" she asked. "Anything that might help us figure out this situation?"

Queen Ree and the crowd waited silently for several moments, but no one spoke. No one had anything to add.

"Well, then," the queen said. She turned back to Vidia. "I have no choice. The crown is special to all of us. It doesn't belong to me. It belongs to Pixie Hollow. If we should find that anyone here has taken it, that would be very serious." She took a deep breath before continuing. "I think we would have to call it an act of treason," she said sadly. "And the only fitting punishment for such a crime . . . is lifetime banishment from Pixie Hollow."

Vidia's mouth dropped open in shock. "This is unbelievable!" she cried. "This is so unfair! Don't I even get a chance to defend myself? Can't I prove that I didn't do it?"

"Of course you can," Queen Ree replied. "But not tonight. It's late. We're all tired." The queen took to the air. She hovered above the crowd. "Let's all gather again the day after tomorrow," she added. "We'll hold Vidia's hearing then, midmorning. Everyone who wishes to come may do so. And, Vidia, you will have the chance to speak to the charges against you." Queen Ree nodded solemnly and brought the meeting to a close. "In the meantime, if anyone learns anything that might help us find the crown, please let me know. Thank you all for coming. Good night."

With that, the queen flew off and inside the Home Tree.

One by one, the other fairies and sparrow men also flew away. Many of them, passing Vidia on their way out of the courtyard, shot her disgusted looks. Others avoided looking at her altogether.

3

VIDIA WAS STILL in shock. She sat on the ground in the shadows of a mulberry bush and stared blankly ahead of her. She made no move to go until it seemed she was all alone. Then, with a heavy sigh, she stood up and turned around—and saw Prilla sitting on a toadstool on the far side of the courtyard.

Kindhearted Prilla was one of the youngest Never fairies. She was fairly new

to Pixie Hollow. She hadn't known Vidia as
long as others had. But she had spent more
time with Vidia than many of them. That
was because Prilla, along with Vidia and
Rani, had been chosen by Mother Dove to

go on the great quest to save Mother Dove's egg. It hadn't been easy. Rani and Prilla had been forced to work with Vidia as a team for the good of Never Land. And in the end, they had succeeded.

Along the way, Prilla felt she had gotten to know Vidia a little better. Prilla knew why fairies thought Vidia was difficult. Sometimes she was nasty and selfish. She *had* plucked Mother Dove in order to get fresh feathers so she could fly faster. Vidia admitted that. But Prilla had seen another side of Vidia, too. Toward the end of the great quest, Vidia had had to make a choice: she could either share her extra-powerful fairy dust to save Never Land or keep it all for herself while the whole island lost its magic.

Vidia had chosen to share.

Maybe that was part of the reason Prilla stayed behind when the emergency meeting ended. Unlike some of the other fairies, Prilla didn't believe that Vidia was all bad.

"Vidia, are you okay?" Prilla asked. She flew over and landed at the fast-flying fairy's side.

Vidia waved Prilla away. "Oh, save your pity, sweetheart," she replied. She forced a smile, but it quickly faded. "Do you think I'm worried? Well, think again. There's a reason I live on my own in the sour-plum tree. It's because I find all of you very irritating. What do I care if I'm banished from Pixie Hollow? I can't stand the place."

Prilla wasn't buying it. She could see the fear in Vidia's eyes. Oh, she knew that Vidia found Pixie Hollow annoying. But even Vidia wouldn't want to be forced to leave her home and live all alone, away from her own kind, forever.

"I'll help you, Vidia," Prilla offered. "Tomorrow, we'll start an investigation. We can ask around and see if we can find out what *really* happened to the crown. It's like a mystery that needs to be solved, don't you see?" Prilla jumped into the air and turned a somersault. "We'll be detectives!"

Vidia wrinkled her brow and looked sideways at Prilla. "Why do you want to help me?" she asked suspiciously. "And how do you know I *didn't* take the crown?"

Prilla landed and shrugged. "I don't

know," she said. "Maybe you did take it. But I don't think so."

Vidia noticed that Prilla hadn't really answered her first question. "And *why* do you want to help me, dearest?" Vidia asked again.

Prilla thought it over for a moment. When she'd first arrived in Pixie Hollow, she'd had trouble figuring out what her talent was. Talents were a big deal. Fairies spent lots of time with the other members of their talent. They ate meals together. Their best friends were usually members of their talent. Without knowing what her talent was, Prilla had had a hard time finding her place in Pixie Hollow.

In the end, Prilla had learned that she was the first fairy with her particular talent—the first mainland-visiting clapping-talent fairy ever. There were no other members of her talent. But then other fairies had made her an honorary member of their talents. Over time, Prilla had settled into life in Pixie Hollow. She had made lots of new friends. She had found her place.

But she still remembered those early days.

Prilla looked Vidia in the eye. "I want to help you," she said, "because I remember what it's like to feel alone."

Vidia returned Prilla's gaze. For a long moment they stared at each other. Vidia never asked for help and she wasn't used to getting any. She wasn't sure what to say.

Vidia looked away. She cleared her

throat. She looked up at the stars. She cleared her throat again.

"Okay" was all she said at last.

It was barely a whisper. But Prilla heard it, and she understood.

VIDIA AND PRILLA met after breakfast in the lobby of the Home Tree the next morning.

"Vidia!" Prilla exclaimed as the fast-flying fairy zipped through the front door. Prilla was eager to share with Vidia all the ideas she had for kicking off their investigation. She had come up with a list of fairies they could question, leads they could follow. "Vidia, I've been thinking—"

"Thinking?" Vidia said. She cut Prilla off and flew right past her. Prilla had to rush to catch up. "Now, why would you go and start experimenting with that?" Vidia asked snippily.

Clearly, Vidia wasn't going to be nice to Prilla just because Prilla had offered to help her. "Come on," Vidia barked. "We'll start by questioning the queen's helper fairies."

Prilla struggled to keep up as she followed Vidia to the second floor of the Home Tree. They turned down the southeastern hallway and soon flew up to the door to Room 10A, where Queen Ree lived.

Vidia knocked loudly on the door. When no one answered right away, she impatiently knocked again, more loudly.

Cinda opened the door. She peeked out into the hall.

"Ah, Cinda," said Vidia. She brushed past her into the queen's sitting room without waiting to be invited in. "What a brave little fairy you were last night, darling— coming forward to tell your tale in front of that big, scary crowd." Vidia flashed Cinda a sickly sweet smile. "But we have just a few more questions to ask you and your fellow helper fairies. Don't we, Prilla?"

Prilla hadn't gotten any farther than the doorway. She had never been inside the queen's rooms before. She stood gazing at the elegant surroundings. The sitting room had pale peach walls, overstuffed sofas, and a floral carpet. Beyond the sitting room were the sea green walls of the queen's bedroom.

Prilla could see one corner of a large, high four-poster bed.

The three other helper fairies, Rhia, Lisel, and Grace, flew out from the queen's bedroom. They were carrying a pile of the softest spiderweb bed linen. They landed abruptly when they saw Vidia.

"What's *she* doing here?" Lisel asked Cinda with a sneer. Rhia and Grace also eyed Vidia warily. It was obvious that they thought she was guilty of stealing the crown.

Prilla flew forward and tried to smooth things over. "We'd just like to ask you some questions about yesterday," she said hopefully, "so we can prepare Vidia's defense for tomorrow."

"*We?*" said Grace, her eyes wide with

surprise. "Prilla, are you actually *helping* her?"

Prilla shrugged and her glow flared. "Yes," she replied. "There's no proof that Vidia took the crown."

"No proof *yet*," Lisel muttered under her breath. She turned away and led Grace, Rhia, and Cinda over to a large table on the far side of the sitting room. They set the sheets and pillowcases on the table and began folding them.

"Listen, dearies," Vidia said. She flew across the room to hover over the helper fairies as they folded. "All I want to know is when each of you last saw the crown. It is your duty, as the queen's helper fairies, to take care of all of her belongings, right? But perhaps in this case, you lost track of a certain something? Perhaps you don't remember when you last saw the crown?"

The helper fairies' pride rose to Vidia's challenge.

"Of course we remember!" Grace protested. "The last time I saw the crown was the day before yesterday, in the evening. I put it back into the crown cabinet after Queen Ree wore it down to dinner."

Lisel nodded. "That's right," she said. She added a folded bedsheet to the growing pile. "I saw Grace put it away that evening. I was here in the room when she did it. That was the last time I saw the crown."

Cinda shook the wrinkles out of a pillowcase. "I saw the crown yesterday morning," she said. "Rhia took it out of the cabinet to make sure it was ready for the party. Right, Rhia?"

"Right," Rhia replied. "I took the crown out and started to clean it. Then I noticed that there was a small dent in the metal." Rhia looked around at her fellow helper fairies. "Well, I didn't think it was right for the queen to have a dent in her

crown at her own party." The other fairies nodded. "So I took the crown up to the crown-repair workshop to have it fixed."

Vidia zipped excitedly to Rhia's side. "And when was this?" Vidia asked.

"Yesterday morning," Rhia said. She described how she had put the crown in its black velvet carrying pouch, taken it up to the crown-repair workshop, and left it with Aidan, the crown-repair sparrow man. "I told him what needed to be fixed. I told him it was a rush. And I asked him to bring it back to the queen's chambers when he was done."

"I see," Vidia replied. "And he did? He brought it back?"

Rhia nodded confidently. "Yes," she said. Then her brow wrinkled. "I mean, I think so." Her glow flared. "Well, actually, I don't know for *sure*."

The three other helper fairies stopped folding. They stared at Rhia. "Rhia," said Lisel in shock, "what do you mean you don't know for *sure*?"

"Well . . . I . . . I mean," Rhia stammered, "I told him I might not be here when he brought it back. I would be in and out. I told him he could leave it with any one of us, whoever was here." Rhia's eyes searched her friends' faces. "Didn't any of you see him bring it back yesterday?" she asked hopefully.

Lisel shook her head.

"Not me," said Grace.

"Me neither," said Cinda.

Rhia covered her mouth with her

hand. It muffled the sound when she cried, "Oh, no!"

Prilla shot Vidia an "aha!" look. "Well, if Rhia took the crown to Aidan," Prilla said, "and none of you saw the crown after that . . ."

Vidia zipped toward the door. "Come on, Prilla," she called behind her. "We have a crown-repair sparrow man to visit."

By the time Prilla caught up with Vidia on the fifth floor of the Home Tree, Vidia was already questioning Aidan in the crown-repair workshop.

"What do you mean you didn't see the crown yesterday?" Vidia was shouting. She hovered over Aidan while he sat at his workbench. "Rhia said she brought it to you to be fixed!"

"I did!" exclaimed a voice behind Prilla. She turned to find Rhia standing in the doorway of the workshop. Prilla didn't realize that Rhia had followed her up from the queen's rooms. She had wanted to hear Aidan's side of the story, too.

Aidan nervously scratched his ginger-colored hair. He looked shocked. Moments before, he'd had his quiet workshop all to himself—as he did most days. Aidan's talent was a specialized one. There weren't many crowns in Pixie Hollow in need of repair. In fact, there weren't many crowns in Pixie Hollow at all! So most of Aidan's time was spent on his own, perfecting his crown-repair skills.

As a result of his lonely work, Aidan was quite shy. Even from far away, Vidia scared him. Now, suddenly, here she was, hovering over him and shouting.

"Please," said Aidan. He held up his hands in surrender. "I—I'm telling you the truth. I saw *Rhia* yesterday, but I d-didn't see the queen's crown."

Rhia flew across the workshop and landed at Aidan's side. "Don't you remember?" she asked. She described again how she had come into the workshop on the previous day. She had asked Aidan to fix the dent in the crown, told him it was a rush, and left the crown there. "I asked you to bring it back to the queen's chambers when you were done," she said. "So why didn't you?"

Aidan's big green eyes had grown wider as Rhia told her story. "Is *that* why you came into my workshop yesterday?" he asked her. "Rhia, when you came in yesterday, I had just finished doing some work with my gemstone drill." Aidan reached across his workbench. He picked up a tool that looked like a cross between a hand mixer and a screwdriver. "It works well, but it makes a terrible racket. Here, I'll show you."

Aidan took a piece of quartz from a pile of stones to his left. He aimed the drill bit into the quartz with one hand. He turned the drill's crank with the other. A deafening, high-pitched squeal filled the workshop. Vidia, Prilla, and Rhia covered their ears with their hands.

"Stop, stop, stop!" Vidia shouted over the noise. Aidan stopped drilling.

Prilla uncovered her ears. "Gosh, Aidan," she said. "How do you stand it?"

Aidan reached into the pockets of his baggy work pants. "I use these," he replied, pulling his hands out of his pockets. He opened them to reveal several wads of dandelion fluff. Then he stuffed a wad in each ear to show how it worked.

"Let's cut to the chase," Vidia snapped impatiently. "What does all this have to do with the missing crown?"

"WHAT?" said Aidan loudly.

Vidia sighed and yanked the fluff out of his ears. "WHY DO I CARE ABOUT YOUR EARPLUGS?" she shouted.

Aidan shrank from Vidia. He turned toward Rhia instead. "Well, when you came in yesterday, I had my back to you. Didn't I?"

Rhia nodded.

"I still had the dandelion fluff in my ears," said Aidan, "because I was working with the drill." He shrugged. "So whatever you said, I didn't hear. When I turned and saw you standing in the doorway, I waved. Remember? But then you turned and left! So I figured you had just dropped by to say hello."

Rhia held her head in her hands. "And *I* thought you were waving to show that you had heard everything I'd said." She groaned. Then an idea came to her. "But whether you heard me or not, I *did* leave the crown here." She flew over to a tree-bark table near the door of the workshop. She pointed to a specific spot on the table. "It was in its black velvet carrying pouch. I put it right here." But there was no sign of the

crown or the pouch anywhere on the table—
just a jumble of scrap metal that Aidan had
tossed into a pile.

"Well," said Prilla hopefully, "maybe
it's around here somewhere." She peeked
under the table. Rhia checked inside some
nearby cupboards.

But there was no crown or velvet pouch to be found.

Prilla sighed. "Aidan," she said, "did anyone else come into your workshop yesterday? Anyone besides Rhia?"

Aidan thought it over, then nodded. "Yes. Twire came by," he replied.

"Twire?" said Rhia. "The scrap-metal-recovery fairy?"

Aidan nodded again. He pointed to the pile of scrap metal on the table next to the door. "She picked up yesterday's scrap metal. She melts it down and recycles it."

Prilla gasped.

Rhia groaned.

Vidia pursed her lips and shook her head.

"What?" said Aidan.

Vidia flashed Aidan her sickly sweet smile. "Don't you see, pet?" she said. "If the crown was on that table next to the scrap metal when Twire came to pick it up . . ."

"She might have taken the crown away with the metal. . . ." Rhia continued the thought.

Prilla gulped. "And melted it down!"

6

"FLY, VIDIA, FLY!" Prilla called out. And the fastest fast-flying-talent fairy in Pixie Hollow rocketed out of Aidan's workshop and zipped toward Twire's.

As she flew, Vidia wondered why she cared so much about saving the queen's crown. *So what if I'm too late? So what if the hunk of junk has been melted down?* she thought. *What do I care? I've already got at least two other fairies I can link to the crown's disappearance—Rhia and Aidan.*

Surely Queen Ree would not banish her after hearing what Rhia and Aidan had to say.

Still, Vidia raced on toward Twire's workshop. She told herself it was because it would be easier to clear her name if she found the crown. But . . . was there a part of Vidia that actually *did* care about one of Pixie Hollow's oldest treasures?

Twire's scrap-metal workshop was on the third floor of the Home Tree. In her rush, Vidia barged through the door without knocking and flew straight into a set of metal wind chimes that hung from the ceiling.

Prrriiinnnnnngggggg! The wind chimes

rang forcefully as Vidia plowed through them. Across the workshop, a startled Twire straightened up and took a break from her task—dropping bits of scrap aluminum and copper into a large vat of molten metal.

"Stop!" Vidia called out. "Stop what you're doing!"

Twire took off her sea-glass safety goggles and wiped them on her coveralls. "What's the matter?" she replied in a calm tone, putting the goggles back on.

Twire was the type of fairy who always saw the glass as half full. She found the hope in every situation—even the most dire—the same way she saw beauty in each piece of scrap metal, no matter how twisted or rusted. Twire had a passion for turning trash into beautiful items. They were all over her workshop: the wind chimes by the door, the flying-fairy mobile by the window, the lamp on the workbench. They were all crafted from scrap metal.

Twire also believed that most bad situations could be turned into good situations. So as Vidia began madly sorting through the pile of metal Twire was melting down, Twire tried to calm her.

"Whatever it is, Vidia, I'm happy to help. Just tell me what's going on," Twire offered.

Just then Prilla arrived, slightly out of breath. She watched as Vidia tossed a piece of copper over her shoulder. It landed with a clang on the workshop floor. "The queen's crown!" Vidia snapped. "Have you seen it?"

Twire shook her head. "No, Vidia. I haven't," she replied calmly. "What makes you think it's here?" She turned to Prilla. "Hello, Prilla," she said kindly. "Are you here with Vidia?"

Twire looked surprised when Prilla nodded, but she didn't say anything.

Vidia gave up her search and sighed an

annoyed sigh. She impatiently repeated what Aidan had said: that Twire had picked up his scrap metal the day before.

Twire nodded. "That's right," she said. "I pick up Aidan's scrap metal every day. Yesterday I brought it back here, sorted it, and began to melt some pieces down."

Prilla watched as Vidia leaned over Twire menacingly. "And you're sure you didn't find anything unusual mixed in with the metal?" she asked. "Think carefully, love. The crown might have been in a black velvet pouch."

At this, Twire started. "Velvet?" she said, her face brightening. "Yes! Yes, I did find some velvet in the pile." She smiled and patted Vidia on the back. "You see," she said encouragingly, "we're on the right track. We'll figure this out."

"Oh, cut it out!" Vidia snapped impatiently. She shook Twire's hand off her back. "Just tell me what you did with it!"

Twire sighed. Vidia was a very negative fairy! Twire flew toward a tiny door in the wall at the far side of the workshop. Vidia and Prilla followed.

"Well, I didn't know it was a pouch," Twire explained as she flew. "I didn't feel anything inside it. But Queen Ree's crown is just about the lightest and most delicate thing ever made. That's probably why I thought it was a piece of unwanted fabric." Twire shrugged. "I was sure I could use it for something. But it had a few rust stains on it. You know, from being tossed around with the metal."

Twire pulled open a small, square door

in the wall. It opened onto a metal chute that dropped down and away into total darkness. "I tossed it down the laundry chute with my other laundry," she said.

7

Vidia took off so suddenly, Prilla had to fly her fastest to catch up. So fast, in fact, that when Vidia paused for a moment on the Home Tree's central staircase between the third and second floors, Prilla bumped into her and fell over backward.

"Oof!" Prilla cried.

"Watch where you're flying!" Vidia shouted. She threw Prilla a dirty look before flying on toward the first floor, where the laundry room was.

Prilla followed. "Well," she called after Vidia, "at least Twire didn't melt the crown down!"

"That's right," snapped Vidia over her shoulder. "She didn't melt it down. No such luck."

Prilla shook her head as she and Vidia flew to the laundry room. At the bottom of the staircase, they turned down the hall that led to the kitchen. Then, dodging the cooking-, baking-, and dishwashing-talent fairies, they flew through the kitchen and into another hallway. At the far end was a swinging door with a small round window.

Pushing through the door, Vidia and Prilla found themselves in the Home Tree laundry room. It was a huge room with towering fifteen-inch ceilings. The whitewashed walls and overhead lights made it seem like the brightest and cleanest room ever. Busy laundry-talent fairies and sparrow men flew this way and that. Some carried baskets of dirty laundry to the rows of washtubs, where other fairies were scrubbing away. Some pushed balloon carriers—carts

kept aloft by fairy-dust-filled balloons—full of wet laundry. Still others stood before long tables, folding clean laundry.

Hundreds of laundry chutes carried laundry down to the laundry room floor from the workshops and bedrooms on the floors above. The dirty laundry fell into baskets. Each chute was marked with the floor number and room it came from.

Vidia and Prilla found the laundry chute labeled 3G. It was the chute that led down from Twire's workshop. A laundry fairy named Lympia was standing under it, sorting through some clothing in a basket. Prilla asked her if she had worked at the same chute the day before. When Lympia said yes, Vidia launched into her questioning.

"Did you find anything . . . *unusual* in

Twire's laundry yesterday afternoon?" she asked pointedly.

"What do you mean, unusual?" Lympia replied. She eyed Vidia suspiciously. Like the queen's helper fairies, Lympia didn't trust Vidia. "Prilla, what's this all about?" she asked.

"We're on the trail of the missing crown," Prilla explained. She gave Lympia a rundown of what they had found out so far. She told her how Rhia had taken the crown to Aidan's workshop and how it had been accidentally picked up by Twire. And then how Twire had dropped it down her laundry chute without knowing it.

"Are you sure you didn't find a black velvet pouch mixed in with Twire's laundry yesterday?" Prilla asked Lympia.

Lympia started. "Oh!" she exclaimed. "Well, yes, I did find a velvet something-or-other. But what does that have to do with anything?"

Vidia sighed. "The crown was *inside* the pouch, precious," she said, sounding annoyed. "Honestly, if anyone had bothered to look inside the thing, I wouldn't be in this mess!"

Rolling her eyes at Vidia, Lympia turned again to Prilla. "I was going through Twire's laundry, sorting it into lights and darks," she explained. "When I found the piece of velvet, I put it aside. It couldn't be washed in the laundry, you see. It had to be cleaned specially."

Prilla nodded. That made sense. "So where did you put it?" Prilla asked.

There was a long pause as Lympia

thought it over. "You know," she said at last, "I really couldn't say."

Vidia smirked. "Well, that's fine," she said in a falsely casual tone. She shrugged. "Tomorrow at my hearing, I'll just say that we traced the crown as far as the laundry room. But then we hit a dead end. Because Lympia *really couldn't say* where she had put Pixie Hollow's most prized possession!" Vidia turned as if to fly away. "This is a waste of time."

Lympia's glow flared. "No! Wait!" she called.

Vidia stopped in her tracks and turned around.

"Let me try to retrace my steps," Lympia suggested to Prilla. "Maybe that will help me remember what happened to the velvet pouch."

So Vidia and Prilla followed her to the balloon carrier storage area. "Yesterday afternoon, after I sorted Twire's laundry, I picked up a balloon carrier and put the laundry inside," Lympia said. She pulled out one of the carriers to show them. "The light clothes were in one basket. The darks were in another basket. And I laid the velvet pouch in the bottom of the carrier."

They followed her as she pushed the balloon carrier over to the washtubs. "Then I put Twire's lights in the wash," Lympia went on. "I left the basket by the tubs."

They followed her to the sinks. "Here I scrubbed some of the stains on one of the darks."

They followed her back to the washtubs. "I put Twire's darks in the water. I left the basket in front of the tub while I cleaned them."

They followed her to the balloon carrier storage area. "Then I brought the balloon carrier back here," said Lympia. She tied up the one she had borrowed again. "And I took a break while the wash was soaking."

Lympia put a hand to her forehead. "I guess I forgot to take the velvet pouch out of the carrier before I returned it," she said sheepishly.

8

LYMPIA HAD NO idea who had used that balloon carrier next. But she did have one more piece to add to the puzzle.

"Yesterday lots of laundry-talent fairies were washing and folding tablecloths for the queen's Arrival Day party," Lympia remembered. "They loaded all the clean tablecloths and napkins into balloon carriers. Then the celebration-setup fairies came to pick them up." Lympia shrugged. "Maybe one of them took the carrier with the pouch in it—hidden under the clean laundry?" she suggested.

Prilla thanked Lympia for her help. Vidia was already halfway across the room, headed for the door.

"Hey, Vidia! Wait up!" Prilla called as she chased after her.

Vidia waited outside the laundry room for Prilla. "We've been at this all morning!" Vidia fumed. "And we're no closer to finding the crown!"

Prilla smiled. She patted Vidia on the back. "Sure we are," Prilla said encouragingly. "We're hot on the trail! We're putting all the pieces together! We're solving the mystery!" Prilla's blue eyes twinkled. "And you've got to admit—it is kind of fun."

Vidia pursed her lips and squinted at Prilla. Then, without a word, she turned and zipped off down the corridor. But before she did, Prilla thought she saw a tiny twinkle in Vidia's eye, too.

They tracked down the celebration-setup fairies in the tearoom. When they weren't setting up for a big party, they helped the kitchen fairies with the setup of meals. As Prilla and Vidia entered the tearoom, some were setting the tables for lunch. Others were carrying dishes and trays out of the kitchen and placing them on a buffet table.

Prilla's stomach growled. She knew that she might not have the chance to eat for the rest of the afternoon. So she helped

herself to a strawberry angel food cupcake from the buffet.

Then, her mouth full, she spotted Vidia already talking to Nora, one of the celebration-setup fairies. Prilla flew over in time to hear Vidia's question.

"Excuse me, honey lamb," said Vidia. She turned on the sweetness. "But did you find a black velvet pouch when you were setting up for the party yesterday? It was mixed in with the tablecloths."

Nora was laying out forks and knives on one table. Without even looking up, she replied, "You mean the velvet pouch with the crown inside it?"

Vidia and Prilla couldn't believe their ears. Did Nora know where the crown was? And if she did, why hadn't she said anything at the emergency meeting?

Vidia spoke first. "Yes! Yes!" she cried. "The one with the crown inside it! Nora, where is it?"

Nora looked up. She was taken aback by the excitement in Vidia's voice. "Well, we took it out of the pouch and tossed it in the back room with all the other crowns," she said casually.

Now Vidia and Prilla were *really* confused. "What other crowns?" Prilla asked.

"The crowns for the party," Nora replied. She put the spoons down on the table in a pile. Then she flew away and waved for Vidia and Prilla to follow. "Come on. I'll show you."

Nora led them out of the tearoom and into the dining hall, where the party would have been the night before. A balloon arch still framed the doorway. The tables were still draped in gold and lacy spiderwebs. Everything was ready for the party that hadn't happened.

In the far corner of the dining hall was a small door marked STOREROOM. Nora flew directly to it and opened the door. Then she stood to one side to let Vidia and Prilla go in first.

The room was dimly lit by natural light from one small window high on the wall. At first, Vidia and Prilla could only just make out the rough outline of items in piles on the floor.

Then, as their eyes adjusted to the light, the forms became clearer.

There before them were stacks and stacks of shiny, glittering crowns—and every one of them looked exactly like Queen Ree's!

9

"THEY LOOK GOOD—almost real. Don't they?" Nora said proudly. She pointed to the crowns piled in the storeroom.

"What?" Prilla replied. Her head was spinning.

"What do you mean, '*almost real*'?" Vidia asked.

Nora picked up a crown from one of the piles. "Well, they're fakes, of course," she began. "For the Arrival Day party, we had them made to look just like Queen Ree's real crown. Yesterday evening we were going to put one at each seat. Each fairy could wear it during the party and take it home as a party favor!" Nora smiled and put the fake crown on her head. "Good idea, huh?" she added.

Vidia and Prilla said nothing. They just stared at the fake crowns with wide eyes. So Nora went on.

"But when the queen announced that the real crown was missing"—Nora shot a quick glance at Vidia—"and the party was called off, we left them here." Nora took the crown off her head. She put it back on a pile. "Now we're not sure what to do with them."

Vidia sighed. "Well," she said, "I'll tell you the first thing to be done with them."

Nora looked at Vidia. "What?" she said.

"We'll need to go through them all and look for the real crown," Vidia replied.

Now Nora looked confused. Prilla explained everything—from Rhia's dropping off the dented crown at Aidan's to Lympia's leaving the crown in the pouch in her balloon carrier.

Nora's eyes widened in shock. "But that means . . ." Her voice trailed off as she put the pieces together. "The crown in the velvet pouch . . . the one we tossed in here . . ."

Prilla and Vidia nodded. Yes, the queen's real crown—an irreplaceable work of art from the earliest days of Pixie Hollow—was here. It was somewhere in this dark, dusty storeroom.

How in the world would they find it, mixed in with hundreds of fake crowns that looked exactly like it?

"Nora," Prilla said at last, "who made the fake crowns? Who figured how to copy the real thing so well?"

"Dupe," Nora replied. "You know, he's one of the art talents. He spent a lot of time getting it just right."

A short while later, a gloomy Dupe stood in the storeroom, in the middle of piles and piles of crowns. Prilla, Vidia, and Nora had just filled him in on the problem.

"Well, I worked so hard trying to make

the fake crowns look just like the queen's," Dupe said to the fairies in a sad tone. "And now we're all wishing I hadn't done such a good job."

Poor Dupe! He *had* worked hard on the crown party favors. Then the party had been called off. Now it looked as though the crowns might never be used.

But Vidia wasn't in a sympathetic mood. She wasn't looking forward to their task. Sifting through all the fake crowns would be like looking for a needle in a haystack. "So," she said impatiently to Dupe, "is there a way to tell the real crown from the fakes?"

Dupe nodded. "There is," he replied. "But not by looking at them." He picked up a crown. "You see the delicate metalwork? These rows of moonstones? The large fire opal in the center?" He pointed out all the crown's beautiful features. "When I crafted the fake crowns, I used tin scraps and fake jewels for all of these things. But with a lot of fairy dust and some special magic, I glossed over all the imperfections. There is no way to tell that they aren't real."

The fairies looked carefully at the crown Dupe was holding. It was true. None of them would have guessed that it wasn't the real thing.

But when Dupe said the word "imperfections," Prilla had an idea. "Wait!" she said. "What about the dent? There was a dent in the real crown that Rhia wanted to have fixed. Can't we just look for the crown with the dent?" Prilla asked Dupe. "That one will be the real one, won't it?"

Dupe shook his head. "I'm afraid not,"

he said. "I copied the real crown exactly—dent and all." He pointed to a dent on the fake crown he was holding. "Of course, in time the magic will wear off," he went on. "The fake crowns will look like what they really are: just some scraps of metal with hunks of quartz and colored pebbles stuck onto them."

But that wouldn't happen for months. They needed to find the real crown now!

"There was only one part of the real crown that I wasn't able to copy," Dupe added.

The fairies' faces brightened as Dupe went on.

"When it's placed on someone's head, the real crown magically changes its size to fit the wearer perfectly," he explained. "My magic wasn't strong enough to do that.

All of the fake crowns are size five."

As it turned out, none of them had size 5 heads. Prilla and Nora were both size 4. Dupe was a size 6. Vidia was a size 3½.

At that, Vidia laughed scornfully. "Let me get this straight," she said. "We have to try on all these crowns? Until we find one that magically fits our heads?"

Dupe nodded. "Oh. And one other thing," he said. "There are some words you need to say when you put the crown on your head. The words trigger the real crown's magic."

Vidia eyed him warily. "What kind of words?" she asked. She sounded almost afraid to hear the answer.

Dupe cleared his throat. "You have to say:

"Pixie Hollow,
Mother Dove—
The world we cherish,
The one we love."

Vidia cringed in disgust. "Ugh!" she cried. "That's got to be the sappiest thing I've ever heard!"

Prilla clapped Vidia good-naturedly on the back. "Well, Vidia," she said, "it may not roll off the tongue now. But it will in a few hours—after you've said it a *few hundred times!*"

10

At first, Vidia refused to try on any of the crowns. There was no way she was going to say the magic words. Instead, she made herself comfortable on a flour-filled burlap sack in one corner of the storeroom. She sat there stubbornly, with her arms crossed, watching Prilla, Nora, and Dupe try on crowns and say the verse.

But before long, Vidia grew impatient—

and bored. She realized that the search would move along faster if she helped.

"For goodness' sake," she snapped. "Can't you go any faster? At this rate, we'll be here all night!" She hopped off the flour sack.

Vidia picked up a crown. She placed it on her size 3½ head. Too large, it slipped down and covered her eyes.

Then, in barely a whisper, Vidia said the magic words.

> "*Pixie Hollow,*
> *Mother Dove—*
> *The world we cherish,*
> *The one we love.*"

It pained her to say those corny lines. To make matters worse, nothing happened. Nothing at all. No change. No magic. The crown remained as ill-fitting as ever.

Vidia sighed, took off the crown, and tossed it into the fake pile. Then she picked up another crown and tried again.

This went on through the evening and into the night. It was slow going. At midnight, the unsorted piles still towered higher than the fake pile.

Hours later, as the first light of the new day peeked through the high window, Vidia paused in her search and yawned. She looked around at the others. Dupe was slumped against a box, sound asleep. A crown was perched on his head. Nora's eyes were also closed. She had stretched out on the floor right in the middle of the unsorted crowns.

Prilla, however, kept searching.

Vidia reached for another crown from an unsorted pile. By now, the task was automatic. Reach for crown, place on head, say words, toss. Reach for crown, place on head, say words, toss.

So when it happened, Vidia almost missed it.

Reach for crown, place on head, say words, t—

But this time, as Vidia reached up to take off the crown, she froze.

Was it her imagination? Or had this crown just . . . shrunk?

When she put this one on, it had slipped down and covered her eyes like all the others. But now, as she reached up to touch it, it sat perfectly on the top of her head.

Slowly, Vidia took the crown off. She held it in front of her and stared at it. So this was it. This was Queen Ree's crown. The real thing. Vidia couldn't help giving a sigh of relief. Now she knew for sure that she couldn't be banished from Pixie Hollow. Not only could she prove, beyond a doubt, that she hadn't taken the crown. But she had also figured out exactly how the crown had gone missing—*and* she had tracked it down, too. Yes, Vidia had cleared her name.

She opened her mouth to tell Prilla—then closed it again. A thought was forming in her mind. Her relief had been so strong at first that it had blocked out other very different feelings. But now those other feelings were coming back: anger, bitterness. And something else, too. What was it? A desire for . . . revenge!

Almost everyone in Pixie Hollow had believed Vidia had taken the crown. Now here it was in her hands. She could do whatever she wanted with it. So why *shouldn't* she go ahead and prove everyone right? Why *shouldn't* she steal it? She could probably steal it *and* get away with it! She could hide it from Prilla, Nora, and Dupe. She could show up at her hearing and tell the queen about their investigation—leaving out the part about how she found the real crown in the storeroom. Everyone else's story would cast enough doubt for Vidia to be found not guilty. And yet, she *would* have the real crown!

Vidia hadn't said a word since she had made her discovery. She also had not taken her eyes off the crown.

Now, finally, she looked up and across the room at Prilla.

To Vidia's surprise, Prilla was staring

right at her. In fact, it felt as though Prilla were staring right *through* her.

Prilla knew exactly what was going on in Vidia's head.

In the courtyard of the Home Tree, Queen Ree tried to start the hearing.

"Everyone, please!" she shouted over the noise. "Please, quiet down!"

Slowly but surely, the chitchatting fairies and sparrow men settled down. They had all come to hear what Vidia would say. Just as on the night of the emergency meeting, every spot that was comfortable for sitting—every toadstool and mossy mound—was taken.

Right in front of the Home Tree stood

Queen Ree. A ray of midmorning sun shone down through the leaves and fell on her like a spotlight. At the queen's left, Vidia stood with her hands clasped behind her back.

About ten inches from Vidia, Prilla sat on a toadstool in the front row of the crowd and looked on uneasily.

"Vidia?" Queen Ree said. "This hearing is your chance to speak to the charge against you. You have been charged with the theft of the royal crown." The queen waved Vidia over, letting her take center stage. "Let us all listen with open hearts and open minds to whatever Vidia says."

Queen Ree took several steps back. Vidia came forward, her hands still clasped behind her back.

"Well," Vidia said in a loud, clear voice, "I really don't have anything to say." She took one hand from behind her back and held it out toward the queen. In her hand was the crown. "I think this should speak for itself," Vidia added with a wry smile.

A cry of surprise rippled through the crowd.

"So she *did* take it!" Tinker Bell shouted.

"She admits it!" came another cry from somewhere in the crowd.

"Banish her!" someone else shouted.

Queen Ree stepped forward to speak to the crowd. She held her hands up. "Please!" she cried. "You must stay quiet during the hearing. Otherwise, I will have to hold it in private."

Silence settled over the crowd once more. Queen Ree turned to Vidia. She took the crown from Vidia's hand.

"I don't understand," the queen said. "Don't you want to say anything about where you got this, or why you have it?"

Vidia shook her head. "No," she replied. "But, if it is all right with you, my dear queen"—Vidia smiled sweetly and bowed low before Queen Ree—"I would like to call some others up to say a few words."

The queen nodded. Vidia looked out into the crowd. "I would like to ask Rhia, Aidan, Twire, Lympia, Nora, and Dupe to come up here," she announced.

One by one, the four fairies and two sparrow men flew out of the crowd. Each of them looked somewhat embarrassed as he or she stood next to Vidia.

When all six of them stood facing the crowd, Vidia nodded at Rhia. "Rhia," she said, "be a dear and tell everyone what you did with the crown on the morning of the Arrival Day party."

And so, Rhia began. It was the tale of how the queen's crown went on a long and eventful journey all over the Home Tree. Timidly, Rhia told her part of the story. She had brought the crown to be fixed, and had misunderstood Aidan's wave.

"If only I hadn't been in such a rush," Rhia moaned.

Aidan picked up the story next. He told everyone that his earplugs had kept him from hearing Rhia. He described how Twire must have picked up the crown along with the scrap metal.

And so on and so on . . . The tale was passed from one storyteller to the next—from Aidan to Twire to Lympia to Nora to Dupe. Each one explained his or her role in the disappearance of the crown.

"So once I explained how to tell the difference between the fake crowns and the real one," Dupe said, wrapping up his part of the story, "we all started trying them on." He shrugged and turned to Vidia. "And eventually, Vidia found it. The queen's crown."

And that, it seemed, was the end of the story.

Only Vidia and Prilla knew that one part, toward the end, had been left out. It was the part where Vidia had almost become the evil fairy that many in Pixie

Hollow already thought she was. It was also the part where she had made a better choice.

Vidia sneaked a sideways glance at Prilla. Prilla smiled at her—and a strange thing happened. Vidia smiled back at Prilla. It wasn't one of Vidia's fake, sickly sweet smiles, either. It was a real, true sign of Vidia's gratitude for Prilla's help. Prilla knew there would be no thank-you. She knew that, from this moment on, she and Vidia would probably never speak of the matter again. She knew that the smile was all she would get.

But it was enough.

Queen Ree stepped forward to speak to everyone. "Well," she said, "I think that clears the matter up for me. I have no

doubt that everyone here feels the same."
She glanced around at the crowd. Everyone
nodded in agreement.

"There's just one other thing," the
queen went on. She stepped over to Vidia's
side and laid a hand on her shoulder.
"Vidia, I owe you an apology," she said.
"We all owe you an apology. We accused
you of something you did not do. We also
owe you our thanks. You worked hard to
find the crown and return it safely." Queen
Ree turned to face the crowd. "To celebrate, I'd like to reschedule the party."

The crowd cheered.

"Only, this party will not be an Arrival
Day celebration for me," the queen went
on. "It will be a party for Vidia, too." She
looked questioningly at Vidia. "Will you be

our guest of honor?" the queen asked.

Vidia smiled. "Really, Ree, you flatter me," she said. Her voice dripped with sarcasm. "But, frankly, I'd rather go on another wild-goose chase around the Home Tree, searching for one of your missing baubles, than come to any party of yours." She smiled and took off into the air.

Almost as one, the crowd gasped in shock at Vidia's rudeness. To say such a thing—when the queen had been trying to make everything better!

But then again, Vidia had never been one to mince words.

Read about the most
famous fairy of them all!

The Trouble with Tink

Just then, they heard a metallic creaking sound.
Suddenly—*plink, plink, plink, plink!* One by one,
tiny streams of water burst through the damaged
copper. The pot looked more like a watering can
than something to boil dye in.

"Oh!" Violet and Terence gasped. They
turned to Tink, their eyes wide.

Tink felt herself blush, but she couldn't tear
her eyes away from the leaking pot. She had
never failed to fix a pot before, much less made
it worse than it was when she got it.

The thing was, no fairy ever failed at her talent. To do so would mean you weren't really talented at all.

Don't miss any of the magical
Disney Fairies chapter books!

Beck and the Great Berry Battle

Then, just as Beck flew over the river, she heard
it. A cry. A cry for her? Was someone calling her
name? As she slowed, it got louder.

"Beck! Be-e-e-e-e-eck! Wait! Wait up!" the
voice called.

Beck stopped and hovered in midair. Where
was the call coming from? She looked to the left.
She looked to the right.

She turned to look behind her—and saw a
young hummingbird headed straight for her, at
full speed. He was screaming at the top of his
lungs. "Beck! Help! He-e-e-e-elp!"

Lily's Pesky Plant

Suddenly, something crashed through the leaves over her head. Lily gasped and flew for cover between the roots of a nearby tree. Had a hawk swooped at her? Trembling, Lily peered out from behind the root and scanned the forest.

But there was no sign of a hawk. The forest was still and quiet. Lily looked over at the possum fern and saw that its leaves had uncoiled and turned brown. It had heard the noise and was playing dead.

Then Lily saw something that made her gasp again. In the spot where she had just been standing sat a strange seed.

Rani in the Mermaid Lagoon

Rani's heart thumped wildly in her chest. She knew that the Mermaid Lagoon held many dangers. There were lightning eels, which gave off an electric shock whenever something touched them. There were the small but fierce saberfish, which had teeth that were longer than their fins. And there were tusked Never sharks. These sharks usually left others alone. But when they were angry, they could be ferocious. And, Rani thought, there were probably other dangers, too. Ones she hadn't heard about.

Suddenly, Rani felt certain that the mermaids needed her help.